COLOR

by
Countee Cullen

Ayer Company Publishers, Inc.

Reprint Edition 1999
Ayer Company Publishers, Inc.
Lower Mill Road
North Stratford, NH 03590

ISBN 0-88143-155-9

To my Mother and Father
This First Book

Acknowledgments

FOR permission to reprint certain of these poems thanks is hereby given to the following publications:

The American Mercury
The Bookman
The Century
The Crisis
The Conning Tower: New York World
Folio
Harper's Magazine
Les Continents
The Messenger
The Nation
Opportunity
Palms
Poetry: A Magazine of Verse
The Southwestern Christian Advocate
The Survey Graphic
The World Tomorrow.
Vanity Fair

DURING THE 1920'S, WHEN REAWAKENED INTEREST in Afro-American culture encouraged a so-called "Negro Renaissance," one of the most talented of the new artists was Countee Cullen, who, by the age of 26, had published three volumes of original poetry. For more than thirty years he was one of the best-known and most highly respected Afro-American poets. Praising his smoothly written, melodious verse, established critics—black and white—judged him to be more lyric and impassioned than Paul Laurence Dunbar, more popular than Jean Toomer, and more polished than Langston Hughes.

Born on May 30, 1903, and separated from his mother in early childhood, Cullen was reared in New York City by a Mrs. Porter, whom he identified as his grandmother, and by the Reverend Frederick Cullen, a Methodist minister, who adopted him after Mrs. Porter's death in 1918. In high school and college Cullen distinguished himself in poetry. In 1921, "Life's Rendezvous," a poem which he published in his high school literary magazine, won first prize in a city-wide contest. As a college student at New York University, he won honorable mention in 1923 and 1924 for poems which he entered in the national Bynner Undergraduate Poetry Contest. Finally, in 1925, his poems were unanimously selected for first prize in the contest. By the time he graduated, Phi Beta Kappa, in 1925, he had won additional prizes from several magazines and had published his first book, *Color,* which was both his most representative and his most successful volume of original poetry. Written during a time when Cullen was keenly attracted to Afro-American themes, almost one-third of the book focuses on Afro-Americans.

The volume includes some of his best-known poems: "Yet Do I Marvel," "A Brown Girl Dead," "Incident," "Saturday's Child," "The Shroud of Color," and "Heritage." These reveal characteristic themes and attitudes of Cullen: praise for Afro-Americans, sympathy for their sorrows, and faith in their heritage. In "Incident," Cullen reveals the emotional impact of the sharp slap of discrimination. In "The Shroud of Color," published originally as "Spirit Birth," Cullen evokes a vision of black men to sustain himself spiritually in life's struggles, and in "Heritage," he lyrically employs Jung's theory of subconscious racial memories to explain the impulses and visions which motivate him.

The one-third of *Color* concerned with Afro-Americans should not blind readers to the fact that most of the poems are skillfully written epitaphs, love poems, and poems on various other subjects, which reveal Cullen's realization of the transitory quality of love, sympathy for outcasts, a youthful yearning for death, and occasional despair.

After earning a Master of Arts degree in English from Harvard University in 1926, Cullen accepted a position as an assistant editor for the Urban League's *Opportunity, A Journal of Negro Life,* for which he wrote a monthly literary column, "The Dark Tower." In 1927 he published *Caroling Dusk,* an anthology of poems by Negroes, and two volumes of original poetry—*The Ballad of the Brown Girl* and *Copper Sun.* "The Ballad of the Brown Girl" retells the story of a wealthy brown girl, the descendant of kings, who is murdered by her husband. The poem, which earned honorable mention in the Bynner competition in 1923, had brought Cullen his first significant recognition as a poet. George Lyman Kittredge of Harvard had adjudged it the finest modern rendition of an old ballad that he had ever read. *Copper Sun,* a collection of poems, was also favorably received by critics.

In 1928 Cullen was honored with the first Harmon prize awarded for distinguished achievement in literature by a Negro, and he received a Guggenheim Fellowship. He married Yolande Du Bois, the daughter of W. E. B. Du Bois, and with his fellowship travelled to France, where he intended to

write a series of narrative poems and a libretto for
a musical comedy. The volume which resulted, *The
Black Christ and Other Poems* (1929), was dis-
appointing, even though the title poem is Cullen's
most impressive long poem. "The Black Christ" re-
lates an incident in which Christ returns to substi-
tute himself for a black southern youth pursued
by a lynch mob. The forty-five shorter poems in
the book are generally undistinguished pieces about
occasional topics; many of them painfully reveal
Cullen's deepening bitterness and cynicism, intensi-
fied by his marital unhappiness, which prompted a
divorce in 1930. After his return to America in the
same year, Cullen, rejecting several offers from
southern Negro colleges, accepted a teaching po-
sition in a New York high school.

Although he published an additional volume of
poetry—*The Medea and Some Poems* (1935),
Cullen's most substantial works during his final
years were prose. *One Way to Heaven* (1932) is a
well-written novel about a handsome black rogue
who attempts unsuccessfully to settle into marriage
with an almost fanatically devout wife. The most
interesting material in the novel, however, is
Cullen's satirical depiction of the soirees at which
a Negro hostess entertains the bourgeois and the
intellectuals of Harlem. Of Cullen's two final books
—*The Lost Zoo* (1940), a collection of poems for

children published during the year of his marriage
to Ida Mae Roberson, and *My Lives and How I
Lost Them by Christopher Cat* (1942), the latter
is the more entertaining. A whimsical, sentimental
autobiography of a cat, it delights both children
and adults. At the time of his death in 1946, Cullen
was editing a collection of his poems; this volume
was published posthumously as *On These I Stand*
(1947).

Despite the acclaim accorded Countee Cullen,
his work has disappointed some readers who have
expected, or even demanded, more from the leading
Afro-American poet of his generation. Some of his
contemporaries criticized his failure to assume a
more positive role as spokesman for Afro-Ameri-
cans—to focus his poetry on them, to reveal their
problems, to protest against the restrictions imposed
upon them—in spite of the fact that in his early
poetry Cullen wrote extensively about black Ameri-
cans. He eloquently evoked sympathy and admira-
tion for them, extolled the African heritage, and
protested against the American chauvinism which
today is shown as white racism. Cullen had even
described a compulsion to develop such themes; in
an interview for *The Chicago Bee* (December 29,
1927) he explained: "I find my poetry of itself
treating of the Negro, of his joys and sorrows,
mostly of the latter, and of the heights and depths

of emotion which I feel as a Negro." However, when increasing numbers of critics began to urge Afro-American artists to concentrate on Afro-American themes, he vehemently defended the artist's right to choose his own materials. In *The Crisis* (November, 1929), he argued that black authors have the prerogative to "do, write, create what we will, our only concern being that we do it well and with all the power in us."

Although he sometimes wrote chauvinistically or atavistically about Africans and African-Americans, Cullen was a traditionalist in style. Looking to John Keats and A. E. Housman as models, he imitated the conventions of English and American verse. Rather than experiment, he restricted himself to iambic tetrameter and pentameter, ballad meter, rhymed couplets, and blank verse. Although he generally handled metrics smoothly, he sometimes faltered badly, as in "Two Who Crossed (She Crosses)" or "Pagan Prayer." He admired Keats, but he could not duplicate Keats' sensuosity; Cullen communicated more effectively through images which appeal to the eye or through conceits which delight the mind. He was a craftsman skilled in manipulating deceptively simple phrases; he was an artist who enjoyed irony and deliberate ambiguity.

From the beginning in *Color* to the end of his

poetic career, Cullen was a lyricist, best when writing subjectively and most effective when his feelings derived from subjects sufficiently universal to encourage a reader's interest and, possibly, identification.

Darwin T. Turner
DEAN, GRADUATE SCHOOL
NORTH CAROLINA AGRICULTURAL
AND TECHNICAL STATE UNIVERSITY

Contents

EPITAPHS

FOR LOVE'S SAKE

VARIA

To You Who Read My Book

SOON every sprinter,
 However fleet,
Comes to a winter
 Of sure defeat:
Though he may race
 Like the hunted doe,
Time has a pace
 To lay him low.

Soon we who sing,
 However high,
Must face the Thing
 We cannot fly.
Yea, though we fling
 Our notes to the sun,
Time will outsing
 Us every one.

All things must change
 As the wind is blown;
Time will estrange
 The flesh from the bone.

The dream shall elude
  The dreamer's clasp,
And only its hood
  Shall comfort his grasp.

A little while,
  Too brief at most,
And even my smile
  Will be a ghost.
A little space,
  A Finger's crook,
And who shall trace
  The path I took?

Who shall declare
  My whereabouts;
Say if in the air
  My being shouts
Along light ways,
  Or if in the sea,
Or deep earth stays
  The germ of me?

Ah, none knows, none,
  Save (but too well)
The Cryptic One
  Who will not tell.

This is my hour
   To wax and climb,
Flaunt a red flower
   In the face of time.
And only an hour
   Time gives, then snap
Goes the flower,
   And dried is the sap.

Juice of the first
   Grapes of my vine,
I proffer your thirst
   My own heart's wine.
Here of my growing
   A red rose sways,
Seed of my sowing,
   And work of my days.

(I run, but time's
   Abreast with me;
I sing, but he climbs
   With my highest C.)

Drink while my blood
   Colors the wine,
Reach while the bud
   Is still on the vine. . . .

Then . . .
   When the hawks of death
Tear at my throat
   Till song and breath
Ebb note by note,
   Turn to this book
Of the mellow word
   For a singing look
At the stricken bird.

   Say, "This is the way
He chirped and sung,
   In the sweet heyday
When his heart was young.
   Though his throat is bare,
By death defiled,
   Song labored there
And bore a child."

When the dreadful Ax
   Rives me apart,
When the sharp wedge cracks
   My arid heart,
Turn to this book
   Of the singing me
For a springtime look
   At the wintry tree.

Say, "Thus it was weighed
  With flower and fruit,
Ere the Ax was laid
  Unto its root.
Though the blows fall free
  On a gnarled trunk now,
Once he was a tree
  With a blossomy bough."

Color

Yet Do I Marvel

I DOUBT not God is good, well-meaning,
    kind,
And did He stoop to quibble could tell
    why
The little buried mole continues blind,
Why flesh that mirrors Him must some day
    die,
Make plain the reason tortured Tantalus
Is baited by the fickle fruit, declare
If merely brute caprice dooms Sisyphus
To struggle up a never-ending stair.
Inscrutable His ways are, and immune
To catechism by a mind too strewn
With petty cares to slightly understand
What awful brain compels His awful hand.
Yet do I marvel at this curious thing:
To make a poet black, and bid him sing!

A Song of Praise

(*For one who praised his lady's being fair.*)

YOU have not heard my love's dark throat,
  Slow-fluting like a reed,
Release the perfect golden note
  She caged there for my need.

Her walk is like the replica
  Of some barbaric dance
Wherein the soul of Africa
  Is winged with arrogance.

And yet so light she steps across
  The ways her sure feet pass,
She does not dent the smoothest moss
  Or bend the thinnest grass.

My love is dark as yours is fair,
  Yet lovelier I hold her
Than listless maids with pallid hair,
  And blood that's thin and colder.

You-proud-and-to-be-pitied one,
  Gaze on her and despair;
Then seal your lips until the sun
  Discovers one as fair.

4

Brown Boy to Brown Girl

(Remembrance on a hill) *(For Yolande)*

" AS surely as I hold your hand in mine,
     As surely as your crinkled hair belies
The enamoured sun pretending that he dies
While still he loiters in its glossy shine,
As surely as I break the slender line
That spider linked us with, in no least wise
Am I uncertain that these alien skies
Do not our whole life measure and confine.
No less, once in a land of scarlet suns
And brooding winds, before the hurricane
Bore down upon us, long before this pain,
We found a place where quiet water runs;
I held your hand this way upon a hill,
And felt my heart forebear, my pulse grow
     still."

A Brown Girl Dead

WITH two white roses on her breasts,
  White candles at head and feet,
Dark Madonna of the grave she rests;
  Lord Death has found her sweet.

Her mother pawned her wedding ring
  To lay her out in white;
She'd be so proud she'd dance and sing
  To see herself tonight.

To a Brown Girl

(*For Roberta*)

WHAT if his glance is bold and free,
His mouth the lash of whips?
So should the eyes of lovers be,
And so a lover's lips.

What if no puritanic strain
Confines him to the nice?
He will not pass this way again,
Nor hunger for you twice.

Since in the end consort together
Magdalen and Mary,
Youth is the time for careless weather:
Later, lass, be wary.

To a Brown Boy

THAT brown girl's swagger gives a twitch
  To beauty like a queen;
Lad, never dam your body's itch
  When loveliness is seen.

For there is ample room for bliss
  In pride in clean, brown limbs,
And lips know better how to kiss
  Than how to raise white hymns.

And when your body's death gives birth
  To soil for spring to crown,
Men will not ask if that rare earth
  Was white flesh once, or brown.

8

Black Magdalens

THESE have no Christ to spit and stoop
　　To write upon the sand,
Inviting him that has not sinned
　　To raise the first rude hand.

And if he came they could not buy
　　Rich ointment for his feet,
The body's sale scarce yields enough
　　To let the body eat.

The chaste clean ladies pass them by
　　And draw their skirts aside,
But Magdalens have a ready laugh;
　　They wrap their wounds in pride.

They fare full ill since Christ forsook
　　The cross to mount a throne,
And Virtue still is stooping down
　　To cast the first hard stone.

Atlantic City Waiter

WITH subtle poise he grips his tray
  Of delicate things to eat;
Choice viands to their mouths half way,
  The ladies watch his feet

Go carving dexterous avenues
  Through sly intricacies;
Ten thousand years on jungle clues
  Alone shaped feet like these.

For him to be humble who is proud
  Needs colder artifice;
Though half his pride is disavowed,
  In vain the sacrifice.

Sheer through his acquiescent mask
  Of bland gentility,
The jungle flames like a copper cask
  Set where the sun strikes free.

Near White

AMBIGUOUS of race they stand,
   By one disowned, scorned of another,
Not knowing where to stretch a hand,
   And cry, "My sister" or "My brother."

Tableau

For Donald Duff

LOCKED arm in arm they cross the way,
  The black boy and the white,
The golden splendor of the day,
  The sable pride of night.

From lowered blinds the dark folk stare,
  And here the fair folk talk,
Indignant that these two should dare
  In unison to walk.

Oblivious to look and word
  They pass, and see no wonder
That lightning brilliant as a sword
  Should blaze the path of thunder.

Harlem Wine

THIS is not water running here,
   These thick rebellious streams
That hurtle flesh and bone past fear
   Down alleyways of dreams.

This is a wine that must flow on
   Not caring how nor where,
So it has ways to flow upon
   Where song is in the air.

So it can woo an artful flute
   With loose, elastic lips,
Its measurement of joy compute
   With blithe, ecstatic hips.

Simon the Cyrenian Speaks

HE never spoke a word to me,
    And yet He called my name;
He never gave a sign to me,
    And yet I knew and came.

At first I said, "I will not bear
    His cross upon my back;
He only seeks to place it there
    Because my skin is black."

But He was dying for a dream,
    And He was very meek,
And in His eyes there shone a gleam
    Men journey far to seek.

It was Himself my pity bought;
    I did for Christ alone
What all of Rome could not have wrought
    With bruise of lash or stone.

Incident

(*For Eric Walrond*)

ONCE riding in old Baltimore,
    Heart-filled, head-filled with glee,
I saw a Baltimorean
    Keep looking straight at me.

Now I was eight and very small,
    And he was no whit bigger,
And so I smiled, but he poked out
    His tongue, and called me, "Nigger."

I saw the whole of Baltimore
    From May until December;
Of all the things that happened there
    That's all that I remember.

Two Who Crossed a Line

(*She Crosses*)

FROM where she stood the air she craved
  Smote with the smell of pine;
It was too much to bear; she braved
  Her gods and crossed the line.

And we were hurt to see her go,
  With her fair face and hair,
And veins too thin and blue to show
  What mingled blood flowed there.

We envied her a while, who still
  Pursued the hated track;
Then we forgot her name, until
  One day her shade came back.

Calm as a wave without a crest,
  Sorrow-proud and sorrow-wise,
With trouble sucking at her breast,
  With tear-disdainful eyes,

She slipped into her ancient place,
  And, no word asked, gave none;
Only the silence in her face
  Said seats were dear in the sun.

16

Two Who Crossed a Line

(*He Crosses*)

HE rode across like a cavalier,
  Spurs clicking hard and loud;
And where he tarried dropped his tear
  On heads he left low-bowed.

But, "Even Stephen," he cried, and struck
  His steed an urgent blow;
He swore by youth he was a buck
  With savage oats to sow.

To even up some standing scores,
  From every flower bed
He passed, he plucked by threes and fours
  Till wheels whirled in his head.

But long before the drug could tell,
  He took his anodyne;
With scornful grace, he bowed farewell
  And retraversed the line.

17

Saturday's Child

SOME are teethed on a silver spoon,
   With the stars strung for a rattle;
I cut my teeth as the black raccoon—
   For implements of battle.

Some are swaddled in silk and down,
   And heralded by a star;
They swathed my limbs in a sackcloth gown
   On a night that was black as tar.

For some, godfather and goddame
   The opulent fairies be;
Dame Poverty gave me my name,
   And Pain godfathered me.

For I was born on Saturday—
   "Bad time for planting a seed,"
Was all my father had to say,
   And, "One mouth more to feed."

Death cut the strings that gave me life,
   And handed me to Sorrow,
The only kind of middle wife
   My folks could beg or borrow.

The Dance of Love

(*After reading René Maran's "Batouala"*)

ALL night we danced upon our windy hill,
  Your dress a cloud of tangled midnight
    hair,
And love was much too much for me to wear
My leaves; the killer roared above his kill,
But you danced on, and when some star would
      spill
Its red and white upon you whirling there,
I sensed a hidden beauty in the air;
Though you danced on, my heart and I stood
    still.

But suddenly a bit of morning crept
Along your trembling sides of ebony;
I saw the tears your tired limbs had wept,
And how your breasts heaved high, how
      languidly
Your dark arms moved; I drew you close to
      me;
We flung ourselves upon our hill and slept.

19

Pagan Prayer

NOT for myself I make this prayer,
  But for this race of mine
That stretches forth from shadowed places
  Dark hands for bread and wine.

For me, my heart is pagan mad,
  My feet are never still,
But give them hearths to keep them warm
  In homes high on a hill.

For me, my faith lies fallowing,
  I bow not till I see,
But these are humble and believe;
  Bless their credulity.

For me, I pay my debts in kind,
  And see no better way,
Bless these who turn the other cheek
  For love of you, and pray.

Our Father, God, our Brother, Christ—
  So are we taught to pray;
Their kinship seems a little thing
  Who sorrow all the day.

Our Father, God; our Brother, Christ,
 Or are we bastard kin,
That to our plaints your ears are closed,
 Your doors barred from within?

Our Father, God; our Brother, Christ,
 Retrieve my race again;
So shall you compass this black sheep,
 This pagan heart. Amen.

Wisdom Cometh With the Years

NOW I am young and credulous,
  My heart is quick to bleed
At courage in the tremulous
  Slow sprouting of a seed.

Now I am young and sensitive,
  Man's lack can stab me through;
I own no stitch I would not give
  To him that asked me to.

Now I am young and a fool for love,
  My blood goes mad to see
A brown girl pass me like a dove
  That flies melodiously.

Let me be lavish of my tears,
  And dream that false is true;
Though wisdom cometh with the years,
  The barren days come, too.

To My Fairer Brethren

THOUGH I score you with my best,
   Treble circumstance
Must confirm the verdict, lest
   It be laid to chance.

Insufficient that I match you
   Every coin you flip;
Your demand is that I catch you
   Squarely on the hip.

Should I wear my wreaths a bit
   Rakishly and proud,
I have bought my right to it;
   Let it be allowed.

Fruit of the Flower

MY father is a quiet man
　　With sober, steady ways;
For simile, a folded fan;
　　His nights are like his days.

My mother's life is puritan,
　　No hint of cavalier,
A pool so calm you're sure it can
　　Have little depth to fear.

And yet my father's eyes can boast
　　How full his life has been;
There haunts them yet the languid ghost
　　Of some still sacred sin.

And though my mother chants of God,
　　And of the mystic river,
I've seen a bit of checkered sod
　　Set all her flesh aquiver.

Why should he deem it pure mischance
　　A son of his is fain
To do a naked tribal dance
　　Each time he hears the rain?

Why should she think it devil's art
    That all my songs should be
Of love and lovers, broken heart,
    And wild sweet agony?

Who plants a seed begets a bud,
    Extract of that same root;
Why marvel at the hectic blood
    That flushes this wild fruit?

The Shroud of Color

(For Llewellyn Ransom)

"LORD, being dark," I said, "I cannot
    bear
The further touch of earth, the scented air;
Lord, being dark, forewilled to that despair
My color shrouds me in, I am as dirt
Beneath my brother's heel; there is a hurt
In all the simple joys which to a child
Are sweet; they are contaminate, defiled
By truths of wrongs the childish vision fails
To see; too great a cost this birth entails.
I strangle in this yoke drawn tighter than
The worth of bearing it, just to be man.
I am not brave enough to pay the price
In full; I lack the strength to sacrifice.
I who have burned my hands upon a star,
And climbed high hills at dawn to view the
    far
Illimitable wonderments of earth,
For whom all cups have dripped the wine of
    mirth,
For whom the sea has strained her honeyed
    throat

Till all the world was sea, and I a boat
Unmoored, on what strange quest I willed to
      float;
Who wore a many-colored coat of dreams,
Thy gift, O Lord—I whom sun-dabbled
      streams
Have washed, whose bare brown thighs have
      held the sun
Incarcerate until his course was run,
I who considered man a high-perfected
Glass where loveliness could lie reflected,
Now that I sway athwart Truth's deep abyss,
Denuding man for what he was and is,
Shall breath and being so inveigle me
That I can damn my dreams to hell, and be
Content, each new-born day, anew to see
The steaming crimson vintage of my youth
Incarnadine the altar-slab of Truth?

Or hast Thou, Lord, somewhere I cannot see,
A lamb imprisoned in a bush for me?

Not so? Then let me render one by one
Thy gifts, while still they shine; some little
      sun
Yet gilds these thighs; my coat, albeit worn,
Still holds its colors fast; albeit torn,

27

My heart will laugh a little yet, if I
May win of Thee this grace, Lord: on this
      high
And sacrificial hill 'twixt earth and sky,
To dream still pure all that I loved, and die.
There is no other way to keep secure
My wild chimeras; grave-locked against the
      lure
Of Truth, the small hard teeth of worms, yet
      less
Envenomed than the mouth of Truth, will
      bless
Them into dust and happy nothingness.
Lord, Thou art God; and I, Lord, what am I
But dust? With dust my place. Lord, let me
      die."

Across the earth's warm, palpitating crust
I flung my body in embrace; I thrust
My mouth into the grass and sucked the dew,
Then gave it back in tears my anguish drew;
So hard I pressed against the ground, I felt
The smallest sandgrain like a knife, and smelt
The next year's flowering; all this to speed
My body's dissolution, fain to feed
The worms. And so I groaned, and spent my
      strength

Until, all passion spent, I lay full length
And quivered like a flayed and bleeding thing.

So lay till lifted on a great black wing
That had no mate nor flesh-apparent trunk
To hamper it; with me all time had sunk
Into oblivion; when I awoke
The wing hung poised above two cliffs that
       broke
The bowels of the earth in twain, and cleft
The seas apart. Below, above, to left,
To right, I saw what no man saw before:
Earth, hell, and heaven; sinew, vein, and core.
All things that swim or walk or creep or fly,
All things that live and hunger, faint and die,
Were made majestic then and magnified
By sight so clearly purged and deified.
The smallest bug that crawls was taller than
A tree, the mustard seed loomed like a man.
The earth that writhes eternally with pain
Of birth, and woe of taking back her slain,
Laid bare her teeming bosom to my sight,
And all was struggle, gasping breath, and
       fight.
A blind worm here dug tunnels to the light,
And there a seed, racked with heroic pain,
Thrust eager tentacles to sun and rain;

It climbed; it died; the old love conquered me
To weep the blossom it would never be.
But here a bud won light; it burst and
       flowered
Into a rose whose beauty challenged,
       "Coward!"
There was no thing alive save only I
That held life in contempt and longed to die.
And still I writhed and moaned, "The curse,
       the curse,
Than animated death, can death be worse?"

"Dark child of sorrow, mine no less, what art
Of mine can make thee see and play thy part?
The key to all strange things is in thy heart."

What voice was this that coursed like liquid
       fire
Along my flesh, and turned my hair to wire?

I raised my burning eyes, beheld a field
All multitudinous with carnal yield,
A grim ensanguined mead whereon I saw
Evolve the ancient fundamental law
Of tooth and talon, fist and nail and claw.
There with the force of living, hostile hills
Whose clash the hemmed-in vale with clamor
       fills,

With greater din contended fierce majestic
      wills
Of beast with beast, of man with man, in strife
For love of what my heart despised, for life
That unto me at dawn was now a prayer
For night, at night a bloody heart-wrung tear
For day again; for *this,* these groans
From tangled flesh and interlockèd bones.
And no thing died that did not give
A testimony that it longed to live.
Man, strange composite blend of brute and
      god,
Pushed on, nor backward glanced where last
      he trod.
He seemed to mount a misty ladder flung
Pendant from a cloud, yet never gained a rung
But at his feet another tugged and clung.
My heart was still a pool of bitterness,
Would yield nought else, nought else confess.
I spoke (although no form was there
To see, I knew an ear was there to hear),
"Well, let them fight; they *can* whose flesh is
      fair."

Crisp lightning flashed; a wave of thunder
      shook

My wing; a pause, and then a speaking,
    "Look."

I scarce dared trust my ears or eyes for awe
Of what they heard, and dread of what they
        saw;
For, privileged beyond degree, this flesh
Beheld God and His heaven in the mesh
Of Lucifer's revolt, saw Lucifer
Glow like the sun, and like a dulcimer
I heard his sin-sweet voice break on the yell
Of God's great warriors: Gabriel,
Saint Clair and Michael, Israfel and Raphael.
And strange it was to see God with His back
Against a wall, to see Christ hew and hack
Till Lucifer, pressed by the mighty pair,
And losing inch by inch, clawed at the air
With fevered wings; then, lost beyond repair,
He tricked a mass of stars into his hair;
He filled his hands with stars, crying as he
        fell,
"A star's a star although it burns in hell."
So God was left to His divinity,
Omnipotent at that most costly fee.

There was a lesson here, but still the clod
In me was sycophant unto the rod,

And cried, "Why mock me thus? Am I a
    god?"

"One trial more: this failing, then I give
You leave to die; no further need to live."

Now suddenly a strange wild music smote
A chord long impotent in me; a note
Of jungles, primitive and subtle, throbbed
Against my echoing breast, and tom-toms
    sobbed
In every pulse-beat of my frame. The din
A hollow log bound with a python's skin
Can make wrought every nerve to ecstasy,
And I was wind and sky again, and sea,
And all sweet things that flourish, being free.

Till all at once the music changed its key.

And now it was of bitterness and death,
The cry the lash extorts, the broken breath
Of liberty enchained; and yet there ran
Through all a harmony of faith in man,
A knowledge all would end as it began.
All sights and sounds and aspects of my race
Accompanied this melody, kept pace
With it; with music all their hopes and hates

Were charged, not to be downed by all the
      fates.
And somehow it was borne upon my brain
How being dark, and living through the pain
Of it, is courage more than angels have.   I
      knew
What storms and tumults lashed the tree that
      grew
This body that I was, this cringing I
That feared to contemplate a changing sky,
This that I grovelled, whining, "Let me die,"
While others struggled in Life's abattoir.
The cries of all dark people near or far
Were billowed over me, a mighty surge
Of suffering in which my puny grief must
      merge
And lose itself; I had no further claim to urge
For death; in shame I raised my dust-grimed
      head,
And though my lips moved not, God knew I
      said,
"Lord, not for what I saw in flesh or bone
Of fairer men; not raised on faith alone;
Lord, I will live persuaded by mine own.
I cannot play the recreant to these;
My spirit has come home, that sailed the
      doubtful seas."

With the whiz of a sword that severs space,
The wing dropped down at a dizzy pace,
And flung me on my hill flat on my face;
Flat on my face I lay defying pain,
Glad of the blood in my smallest vein,
And in my hands I clutched a loyal dream,
Still spitting fire, bright twist and coil and
       gleam,
And chiselled like a hound's white tooth.
"Oh, I will match you yet," I cried, "to truth."

Right glad I was to stoop to what I once had
       spurned,
Glad even unto tears; I laughed aloud; I
       turned
Upon my back, and though the tears for joy
       would run,
My sight was clear; I looked and saw the
       rising sun.

Heritage

(For Harold Jackman)

WHAT is Africa to me:
Copper sun or scarlet sea,
Jungle star or jungle track,
Strong bronzed men, or regal black
Women from whose loins I sprang
When the birds of Eden sang?
One three centuries removed
From the scenes his fathers loved,
Spicy grove, cinnamon tree,
What is Africa to me?

So I lie, who all day long
Want no sound except the song
Sung by wild barbaric birds
Goading massive jungle herds,
Juggernauts of flesh that pass
Trampling tall defiant grass
Where young forest lovers lie,
Plighting troth beneath the sky.
So I lie, who always hear,
Though I cram against my ear
Both my thumbs, and keep them there,

Great drums throbbing through the air.
So I lie, whose fount of pride,
Dear distress, and joy allied,
Is my somber flesh and skin,
With the dark blood dammed within
Like great pulsing tides of wine
That, I fear, must burst the fine
Channels of the chafing net
Where they surge and foam and fret.

Africa? A book one thumbs
Listlessly, till slumber comes.
Unremembered are her bats
Circling through the night, her cats
Crouching in the river reeds,
Stalking gentle flesh that feeds
By the river brink; no more
Does the bugle-throated roar
Cry that monarch claws have leapt
From the scabbards where they slept.
Silver snakes that once a year
Doff the lovely coats you wear,
Seek no covert in your fear
Lest a mortal eye should see;
What's your nakedness to me?
Here no leprous flowers rear
Fierce corollas in the air;

Here no bodies sleek and wet,
Dripping mingled rain and sweat,
Tread the savage measures of
Jungle boys and girls in love.
What is last year's snow to me,
Last year's anything? The tree
Budding yearly must forget
How its past arose or set—
Bough and blossom, flower, fruit,
Even what shy bird with mute
Wonder at her travail there,
Meekly labored in its hair.
One three centuries removed
From the scenes his fathers loved,
Spicy grove, cinnamon tree,
What is Africa to me?

So I lie, who find no peace
Night or day, no slight release
From the unremittant beat
Made by cruel padded feet
Walking through my body's street.
Up and down they go, and back,
Treading out a jungle track.
So I lie, who never quite
Safely sleep from rain at night—
I can never rest at all

When the rain begins to fall;
Like a soul gone mad with pain
I must match its weird refrain;
Ever must I twist and squirm,
Writhing like a baited worm,
While its primal measures drip
Through my body, crying, "Strip!
Doff this new exuberance.
Come and dance the Lover's Dance!"
In an old remembered way
Rain works on me night and day.

Quaint, outlandish heathen gods
Black men fashion out of rods,
Clay, and brittle bits of stone,
In a likeness like their own,
My conversion came high-priced;
I belong to Jesus Christ,
Preacher of humility;
Heathen gods are naught to me.

Father, Son, and Holy Ghost,
So I make an idle boast;
Jesus of the twice-turned cheek,
Lamb of God, although I speak
With my mouth thus, in my heart
Do I play a double part.

Ever at Thy glowing altar
Must my heart grow sick and falter,
Wishing He I served were black,
Thinking then it would not lack
Precedent of pain to guide it,
Let who would or might deride it;
Surely then this flesh would know
Yours had borne a kindred woe.
Lord, I fashion dark gods, too,
Daring even to give You
Dark despairing features where,
Crowned with dark rebellious hair,
Patience wavers just so much as
Mortal grief compels, while touches
Quick and hot, of anger, rise
To smitten cheek and weary eyes.
Lord, forgive me if my need
Sometimes shapes a human creed.

All day long and all night through,
One thing only must I do:
Quench my pride and cool my blood,
Lest I perish in the flood.
Lest a hidden ember set
Timber that I thought was wet
Burning like the dryest flax,

Melting like the merest wax,
Lest the grave restore its dead.
Not yet has my heart or head
In the least way realized
They and I are civilized.

Epitaphs

For a Poet

I HAVE wrapped my dreams in a silken
cloth,
And laid them away in a box of gold;
Where long will cling the lips of the moth,
I have wrapped my dreams in a silken cloth;
I hide no hate; I am not even wroth
Who found earth's breath so keen and cold;
I have wrapped my dreams in a silken cloth,
And laid them away in a box of gold.

For My Grandmother

THIS lovely flower fell to seed;
   Work gently, sun and rain;
She held it as her dying creed
   That she would grow again.

For a Cynic

BIRTH is a crime
  All men commit;
Life gives them time
To atone for it;
Death ends the rhyme
As the price for it.

For a Singer

DEATH clogged this flute
   At its highest note;
Song sleeps here mute
   In this breathless throat.

For a Virgin

FOR forty years I shunned the lust
  Inherent in my clay;
Death only was so amorous
  I let him have his way.

For a Lady I Know

SHE even thinks that up in heaven
   Her class lies late and snores,
While poor black cherubs rise at seven
   To do celestial chores.

For a Lovely Lady

A CREATURE slender as a reed,
  And sad-eyed as a doe
Lies here (but take my word for it,
  And do not pry below).

For an Atheist

MOUNTAINS cover me like rain,
    Billows whirl and rise;
Hide me from the stabbing pain
In His reproachful eyes.

For an Evolutionist and His Opponent

S HOWING that our ways agreed,
  Death is proof enough;
Body seeks the primal clay,
  Soul transcends the slough.

For an Anarchist

WHAT matters that I stormed and swore?
  Not Samson with an ass's jaw,
Not though a forest of hair he wore,
  Could break death's adamantine law.

For a Magician

I WHOSE magic could explore
  Ways others might not guess or see,
Now am barred behind a door
  That has no "Open Sesame."

For a Pessimist

HE wore his coffin for a hat,
 Calamity his cape,
While on his face a death's-head sat
 And waved a bit of crape.

For a Mouthy Woman

GOD and the devil still are wrangling
    Which should have her, which repel;
God wants no discord in his heaven;
    Satan has enough in hell.

For a Philosopher

HERE lies one who tried to solve
   The riddle of being and breath:
The wee blind mole that gnaws his bones
   Tells him the answer is death.

For an Unsuccessful Sinner

I BOASTED my sins were sure to sink me
  Out of all sound and sight of glory;
And the most I've won for all my pains
  Is a century of purgatory.

For a Fool

ON earth the wise man makes the rules,
And is the fool's adviser,
But here the wise are as the fools,
(And no man is the wiser).

For One Who Gayly Sowed His Oats

MY days were a thing for me to live,
   For others to deplore;
I took of life all it could give:
   Rind, inner fruit, and core.

For a Skeptic

BLOOD-BROTHER unto Thomas whose
Weak faith doubt kept in trammels,
His little credence strained at gnats—
But grew robust on camels.

For a Fatalist

LIFE ushers some as heirs-elect
   To weather wind and gale;
Here lies a man whose ships were wrecked
   Ere he could hoist a sail.

For Daughters of Magdalen

OURS is the ancient story:
   Delicate flowers of sin,
Lilies, arrayed in glory,
   That would not toil nor spin.

For a Wanton

TO men no more than so much cover
　　For them to doff or try,
I found in Death a constant lover:
　　Here in his arms I lie.

For a Preacher

V ANITY of vanities,
   All is vanity; yea,
Even the rod He flayed you with
   Crumbled and turned to clay.

For One Who Died Singing of Death

HE whose might you sang so well
    Living, will not let you rust:
Death has set the golden bell
    Pealing in the courts of dust.

For John Keats,
Apostle of Beauty

NOT writ in water, nor in mist,
    Sweet lyric throat, thy name;
Thy singing lips that cold death kissed
Have seared his own with flame.

For Hazel Hall,
American Poet

SOUL-TROUBLED at the febrile ways
    of breath,
  Her timid breast shot through with faint
      alarm,
"Yes, I'm a stranger here," she said to Death,
  "It's kind of you to let me take your arm."

For Paul Laurence Dunbar

BORN of the sorrowful of heart,
 Mirth was a crown upon his head;
Pride kept his twisted lips apart
 In jest, to hide a heart that bled.

For Joseph Conrad

NOT of the dust, but of the wave
  His final couch should be;
They lie not easy in a grave
Who once have known the sea.
How shall earth's meagre bed enthrall
The hardiest seaman of them all?

For Myself

WHAT'S in this grave is worth your tear;
  There's more than the eye can see;
Folly and Pride and Love lie here
  Buried alive with me.

All the Dead

PRIEST and layman, virgin, strumpet,
  Good and ill commingled sleep,
Waiting till the dreadful trumpet
  Separates the wolves and sheep.

For Love's Sake

Oh, for a Little While
Be Kind

(For Ruth Marie)

OH, for a little while be kind to me
   Who stand in such imperious need of
      you,
And for a fitful space let my head lie
Happily on your passion's frigid breast.
Although yourself no more resigned to me
Than on all bitter yesterdays I knew,
This half a loaf from sumptuous crumbs
      your shy
Reneging hand lets fall shall make me blest.
The sturdy homage of a love that throws
Its strength about you, dawn and dusk, at bed
And board, is not for scorn. When all is said
With final amen certitude, who knows
But Dives found a matchless fragrance fled
When Lazarus no longer shocked his nose?

If You Should Go

LOVE, leave me like the light,
   The gently passing day;
We would not know, but for the night,
   When it has slipped away.

Go quietly; a dream,
   When done, should leave no trace
That it has lived, except a gleam
   Across the dreamer's face.

To One Who Said Me Nay

THIS much the gods vouchsafe today:
    That we two lie in the clover,
Watching the heavens dip and sway,
  With galleons sailing over.

This much is granted for an hour:
    That we are young and tender,
That I am bee and you are flower,
    Honey-mouthed and swaying slender.

This sweet of sweets is ours now:
    To wander through the land,
Plucking an apple from its bough
    To toss from hand to hand.

No thing is certain, joy nor sorrow,
    Except the hour we know it;
Oh, wear my heart today; tomorrow
    Who knows where the winds will blow it?

Advice to Youth

(*For Guillaume*)

SINCE little time is granted here
   For pride in pain or play,
Since blood soon cools before that Fear
   That makes our prowess clay,
If lips to kiss are freely met,
   Lad, be not proud nor shy;
There are no lips where men forget,
   And undesiring lie.

Caprice

"I'LL tell him, when he comes," she said,
  "Body and baggage, to go,
Though the night be darker than my hair,
  And the ground be hard with snow."

But when he came with his gay black head
  Thrown back, and his lips apart,
She flipped a light hair from his coat,
  And sobbed against his heart.

Sacrament

SHE gave her body for my meat,
   Her soul to be my wine,
And prayed that I be made complete
   In sunlight and starshine.

With such abandoned grace she gave
   Of all that passion taught her,
She never knew her tidal wave
   Cast bread on stagnant water.

Bread and Wine

FROM death of star to new star's birth,
   This ache of limb, this throb of head,
This sweaty shop, this smell of earth,
   For this we pray, "Give daily bread."

Then tenuous with dreams the night,
   The feel of soft brown hands in mine,
Strength from your lips for one more fight:
   Bread's not so dry when dipped in wine.

Spring Reminiscence

"MY sweet," you sang, and, "Sweet," I
     sang,
  And sweet we sang together,
Glad to be young as the world was young,
  Two colts too strong for a tether.

Shall ever a spring be like that spring,
  Or apple blossoms as white;
Or ever clover smell like the clover
  We lay upon that night?

Shall ever your hand lie in my hand,
  Pulsing to it, I wonder;
Or have the gods, being jealous gods,
  Envied us our thunder?

Varia

Suicide Chant

I AM the seed
  The Sower sowed;
I am the deed
  His hand bestowed
Upon the world.

Censure me not
  If a rank weed flood
The garden plot,
  Instead of a bud
To be unfurled.

Bridle your blame
  If the deed prove less
Than the bruited fame
  With which it came
From nothingness.

The seed of a weed
  Cannot be flowered,
Nor a hero's deed
  Spring from a coward.

Pull up the weed;
Bring plow and mower;
Then fetch new seed
For the hand of the Sower.

She of the Dancing Feet Sings

(To Ottie Graham)

"AND what would I do in heaven, pray,
   Me with my dancing feet,
And limbs like apple boughs that sway
   When the gusty rain winds beat?

And how would I thrive in a perfect place
   Where dancing would be sin,
With not a man to love my face,
   Nor an arm to hold me in?

The seraphs and the cherubim
   Would be too proud to bend
To sing the faery tunes that brim
   My heart from end to end.

The wistful angels down in hell
   Will smile to see my face,
And understand, because they fell
   From that all-perfect place."

Judas Iscariot

I THINK when Judas' mother heard
His first faint cry the night
That he was born, that worship stirred
Her at the sound and sight.
She thought his was as fair a frame
As flesh and blood had worn;
I think she made this lovely name
For him—"Star of my morn."

As any mother's son he grew
From spring to crimson spring;
I think his eyes were black, or blue,
His hair curled like a ring.
His mother's heart-strings were a lute
Whereon he all day played;
She listened rapt, abandoned, mute,
To every note he made.

I think he knew the growing Christ,
And played with Mary's son,
And where mere mortal craft sufficed,
There Judas may have won.

Perhaps he little cared or knew,
  So folly-wise is youth,
That He whose hand his hand clung to
  Was flesh-embodied Truth;

Until one day he heard young Christ,
  With far-off eyes agleam,
Tell of a mystic, solemn tryst
  Between Him and a dream.
And Judas listened, wonder-eyed,
  Until the Christ was through,
Then said, "And I, though good betide,
  Or ill, will go with you."

And so he followed, heard Christ preach,
  Saw how by miracle
The blind man saw, the dumb got speech,
  The leper found him well.
And Judas in those holy hours
  Loved Christ, and loved Him much,
And in his heart he sensed dead flowers
  Bloom at the Master's touch.

And when Christ felt the death hour creep
  With sullen, drunken lurch,
He said to Peter, "Feed my sheep,
  And build my holy church."

He gave to each the special task
    That should be his to do,
But reaching one, I hear him ask,
    "What shall I give to you?"

Then Judas in his hot desire
    Said, "Give me what you will."
Christ spoke to him with words of fire,
    "Then, Judas, you must kill
One whom you love, One who loves you
    As only God's son can:
This is the work for you to do
    To save the creature man."

"And men to come will curse your name,
    And hold you up to scorn;
In all the world will be no shame
    Like yours; this is love's thorn.
It takes strong will of heart and soul,
    But man is under ban.
Think, Judas, can you play this role
    In heaven's mystic plan?"

So Judas took the sorry part,
    Went out and spoke the word,
And gave the kiss that broke his heart,
    But no one knew or heard.

And no one knew what poison ate
   Into his palm that day,
Where, bright and damned, the monstrous
     weight
   Of thirty white coins lay.

It was not death that Judas found
   Upon a kindly tree;
The man was dead long ere he bound
   His throat as final fee.
And who can say if on that day
   When gates of pearl swung wide,
Christ did not go His honored way
   With Judas by His side?

I think somewhere a table round
   Owns Jesus as its head,
And there the saintly twelve are found
   Who followed where He led.
And Judas sits down with the rest,
   And none shrinks from His hand,
For there the worst is as the best,
   And there they understand.

And you may think of Judas, friend,
   As one who broke his word,

Whose neck came to a bitter end
  For giving up his Lord.
But I would rather think of him
  As the little Jewish lad
Who gave young Christ heart, soul, and limb,
  And all the love he had.

The Wise

(*For Alain Locke*)

DEAD men are wisest, for they know
How far the roots of flowers go,
How long a seed must rot to grow.

Dead men alone bear frost and rain
On throbless heart and heatless brain,
And feel no stir of joy or pain.

Dead men alone are satiate;
They sleep and dream and have no weight,
To curb their rest, of love or hate.

Strange, men should flee their company,
Or think me strange who long to be
Wrapped in their cool immunity.

Mary, Mother of Christ

THAT night she felt those searching hands
    Grip deep upon her breast,
She laughed and sang a silly tune
To lull her babe to rest;

That night she kissed his coral lips
How could she know the rest?

Dialogue

Soul: THERE is no stronger thing than
           song;
       In sun and rain and leafy trees
       It wafts the timid soul along
       On crested waves of melodies.

Body: But leaves the body bare to feed
       Its hunger with its very need.

Soul: Although the frenzied belly writhes,
       Yet render up in song your tithes;
       Song is the weakling's oaken rod,
       His Jacob's ladder dropped from God.

Body: Song is not drink; song is not meat,
       Nor strong, thick shoes for naked feet.

Soul: Who sings by unseen hands is fed
       With honeyed milk and warm, white
           bread;
       His ways in pastures green are led,
       And perfumed oil illumes his head;

His cup with wine is surfeited,
And when the last low note is read,
He sings among the lipless dead
With singing stars to crown his head.

Body: But will song buy a wooden box
The length of me from toe to crown,
To keep me safe from carrion flocks
When singing's done and lyre laid
down?

In Memory of
Col. Charles Young

ALONG the shore the tall, thin grass
    That fringes that dark river,
While sinuously soft feet pass,
    Begins to bleed and quiver.

The great dark voice breaks with a sob
    Across the womb of night;
Above your grave the tom-toms throb,
    And the hills are weird with light.

The great dark heart is like a well
    Drained bitter by the sky,
And all the honeyed lies they tell
    Come there to thirst and die.

No lie is strong enough to kill
    The roots that work below;
From your rich dust and slaughtered will
    A tree with tongues will grow.

To My Friends

YOU feeble few that hold me somewhat
    more
Than all I am; base clay and spittle joined
To shape an aimless whim substantial; coined
Amiss one idle hour, this heart, though
    poor,—
O golden host I count upon the ends
Of one bare hand, with fingers still to
    spare,—
Is rich enough for this: to harbor there
In opulence its frugal meed of friends.
Let neither lose his faith, lest by such loss
Each find insufferable his daily cross.
And be not less immovable to me,
Not less love-leal and staunch, than my heart
    is.
In brief, these fine heroics come to this,
My friends: if you are true, I needs must be.

Gods

I FAST and pray and go to church,
  And put my penny in,
But God's not fooled by such slight tricks,
  And I'm not saved from sin.

I cannot hide from Him the gods
  That revel in my heart,
Nor can I find an easy word
  To tell them to depart:

God's alabaster turrets gleam
  Too high for me to win,
Unless He turns His face and lets
  Me bring my own gods in.

To John Keats, Poet.
At Spring Time[*]

(*For Carl Van Vechten*)

I CANNOT hold my peace, John Keats;
   There never was a spring like this;
It is an echo, that repeats
My last year's song and next year's bliss.
I know, in spite of all men say
Of Beauty, you have felt her most.
Yea, even in your grave her way
Is laid. Poor, troubled, lyric ghost,
Spring never was so fair and dear
As Beauty makes her seem this year.

I cannot hold my peace, John Keats,
I am as helpless in the toil
Of Spring as any lamb that bleats
To feel the solid earth recoil
Beneath his puny legs. Spring beats
Her tocsin call to those who love her,
And lo! the dogwood petals cover

[*] Spring, 1924

Her breast with drifts of snow, and sleek
White gulls fly screaming to her, and hover
About her shoulders, and kiss her cheek,
While white and purple lilacs muster
A strength that bears them to a cluster
Of color and odor; for her sake
All things that slept are now awake.

And you and I, shall we lie still,
John Keats, while Beauty summons us?
Somehow I feel your sensitive will
Is pulsing up some tremulous
Sap road of a maple tree, whose leaves
Grow music as they grow, since your
Wild voice is in them, a harp that grieves
For life that opens death's dark door.
Though dust, your fingers still can push
The Vision Splendid to a birth,
Though now they work as grass in the hush
Of the night on the broad sweet page of the
    earth.

"John Keats is dead," they say, but I
Who hear your full insistent cry
In bud and blossom, leaf and tree,
Know John Keats still writes poetry.

And while my head is earthward bowed
To read new life sprung from your shroud,
Folks seeing me must think it strange
That merely spring should so derange
My mind. They do not know that you,
John Keats, keep revel with me, too.

On Going

(*For Willard Johnson*)

A GRAVE is all too weak a thing
    To hold my fancy long;
I'll bear a blossom with the spring,
    Or be a blackbird's song,

I think that I shall fade with ease,
    Melt into earth like snow,
Be food for hungry, growing trees,
    Or help the lilies blow.

And if my love should lonely walk,
    Quite of my nearness fain,
I may come back to her, and talk
    In liquid words of rain.

Harsh World That Lashest Me

(*For Walter White*)

HARSH World that lashest me each day,
    Dub me not cowardly because
I seem to find no sudden way
    To throttle you or clip your claws.
No force compels me to the wound
    Whereof my body bears the scar;
Although my feet are on the ground,
    Doubt not my eyes are on a star.

You cannot keep me captive, World,
    Entrammeled, chained, spit on, and
        spurned.
More free than all your flags unfurled,
    I give my body to be burned.
I mount my cross because I will,
    I drink the hemlock which you give
For wine which you withhold—and still,
    Because I will not die, I live.

I live because an ember in
   Me smoulders to regain its fire,
Because what is and what has been
   Not yet have conquered my desire.
I live to prove the groping clod
   Is surely more than simple dust;
I live to see the breath of God
   Beatify the carnal crust.

But when I will, World, I can go,
   Though triple bronze should wall me
     round,
Slip past your guard as swift as snow,
   Translated without pain or sound.
Within myself is lodged the key
   To that vast room of couches laid
For those too proud to live and see
   Their dreams of light eclipsed in shade.

Requiescam

I AM for sleeping and forgetting
  All that has gone before;
I am for lying still and letting
  Who will beat at my door;
I would my life's cold sun were setting
  To rise for me no more.